Karen's Birthday

Also in the Babysitters Little Sister series:

Look out for:

Karen's Birthday

Ann M. Martin

Illustrations by Susan Tang

Hippo Books
Scholastic Children's Books
London

Scholastic Children's Books,
Scholastic Publications Ltd,
7-9 Pratt Street, London NW1 0AE, UK

Scholastic Inc.,
730 Broadway, New York, NY 10003, USA

Scholastic Canada Ltd,
123 Newkirk Road, Richmond Hill,
Ontario, Canada L4C 3G5

Ashton Scholastic Pty Ltd,
P O Box 579, Gosford, New South Wales,
Australia

Ashton Scholastic Ltd,
Private Bag 1, Penrose, Auckland,
New Zealand

First published in the US by Scholastic Inc., 1990
First published in the UK by Scholastic Publications Ltd, 1992

Copyright © Ann M. Martin, 1991

ISBN 0 590 55041 1

Typeset by A.J. Latham Ltd, Dunstable, Beds
Printed by Cox & Wyman Ltd, Reading, Berks

BABYSITTERS LITTLE SISTER is a trademark of Scholastic Inc.

10 9 8 7 6 5 4 3

This book is for the Fultons—
Pam and Jim,
Andrew and Patrick

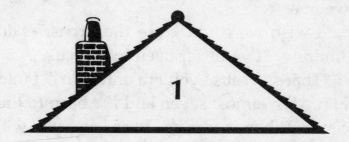

The Happy-Time Circus

"Andrew! Andrew! Here it is again!" I called.

Andrew came flying in from the other room. Andrew is my little brother and he's four. I'm six, *nearly* seven, and I'm his big sister Karen.

"What is it? The Happy-Time Circus?" cried Andrew.

"Yes," I replied.

For a week, Andrew and I had been watching adverts for the Happy-Time Circus. The circus was coming to Stamford,

Connecticut, which isn't too far from where we live.

"I wish we could go to the circus," said Andrew. "I've never been to a circus."

"That's because you are only four," I told him. "I'm almost seven and *I've* been to the circus. When you're as old as I am, you will have done lots of things."

"Did you go to the Happy-Time Circus?" asked Andrew.

"No," I replied, "I went to Doctor Doodle's Big Top."

Andrew and I stood in front of the TV and watched the advert.

"Animals! Animals! Animals!" said the announcer. "Come and see the elephants. Come and see the lions and tigers. Come and see Paddy's Trained Poodles and Biff's Trained Bears."

Andrew and I looked at each other and grinned. We love animals.

"Action! Excitement! Adventure!" the announcer went on. "See death-defying acts on the high wire. See the Cecily Sisters and

2

their trapeze act. See the Balancing Bruno Brothers. See clowns, clowns, and more clowns!"

The announcer told us how you could order tickets and how long the circus would be in Stamford for. Then the advert finished.

"Look at me!" said Andrew. He stood at one end of our playroom. Then he ran forwards and did two somersaults in a row. "I could be an acrobat in the circus," he said. "Or maybe I could be a clown."

"Guess who I am," I said. I stepped carefully across the room. I held my arms out as if I needed them to help me balance.

"You're one of the Balancing Bruno Brothers," said Andrew.

"Right," I replied. "I wish I could be *in* the circus," I added.

"Me, too," said Andrew. "I want to be the man who stands in the middle of the tent and wears a top hat and tall black boots. What's he called again?"

"The ringmaster," I told Andrew

importantly. That's the sort of thing you know when you're almost seven.

Just then the phone rang.

"I'll get it!" I screeched. I ran into the kitchen where Mummy was making dinner.

"Indoor voice, Karen," she reminded me. She has to remind me about that a lot.

"Okay," I answered. I picked up the phone. "Hello?" I said. "This is Karen Brewer."

"Hello, Karen Brewer. This is your father."

"Daddy!" I tried not to shout, but I couldn't help it.

"I'm phoning," said Daddy, "because someone I know has a birthday coming up."

"Me! It's me!"

"Well, I was wondering," Daddy went on, "if you would like to do something special for your birthday. . . . That *is* Karen Brewer, isn't it?"

"Daddy!" I cried again. He likes to tease me. "Yes, this is Karen, and I *do* want to do something special."

I knew just what it was, too.

"Would you like to invite some of your friends to go to the Happy-Time Circus?" asked Daddy. "If you would, I'll get tickets."

The Happy-Time Circus? I was so surprised. That wasn't what I had expected Daddy to say at all.

2

Two of Everything

Of course, there was no way Daddy could have guessed what I wanted to do for my birthday because I hadn't given anybody any hints. I could tell that Daddy really wanted to take my friends and me to the circus. Daddy *loves* circuses, and he knew that I wanted to go to the Happy-Time Circus . . . but not for my birthday.

"Oh, Daddy," I said. I tried to sound excited. "Thank you. The circus would be . . . great. But I haven't thought much about my birthday." That was a *huge* lie as

I had been thinking about my birthday for *ages*. "Can I decide about the circus in a little while?" I asked him.

Daddy said I could take my time deciding, and then we said goodbye. I went to my bedroom and took Emily Junior out of her cage and put her on my lap. Emily Junior is my rat. (She is named after my adopted sister.)

I sat and thought. I thought about my birthday and the circus and being a two-two.

What is a two-two? A two-two is someone like Andrew and me who has two of everything because their parents are divorced. I got the name from a book my teacher read to our class. It was called *Jacob Two-Two Meets the Hooded Fang*. I thought "two-two" described my brother and me perfectly. I am Karen Two-Two and Andrew is Andrew Two-Two.

You see, a long time ago my mummy and daddy used to be married. Then they got divorced and *then* they both got married again. Mummy married Seth who is my

stepfather, and Daddy married Elizabeth who is my stepmother. Andrew and I live with Mummy and Seth most of the time. But every other weekend, and for two weeks during the summer, we live with Daddy and Elizabeth.

Mummy and Seth live in a little house. No one else lives there except Andrew and me, and Rocky and Midgie and Emily Junior (Rocky and Midgie are Seth's cat and dog). So the little house is usually quiet.

Daddy and Elizabeth live in a huge house. in fact, it's a mansion. And it's very noisy because lots of people are always around. For one thing, Elizabeth has four children of her own. They are Sam and Charlie, who are so grown-up they're in high school, and Kristy, who is thirteen and one of my favourite people. (She is a good babysitter as well as a nice stepsister.) There is also David Michael, who's seven. As soon as I have my birthday, we'll be the same age. Then there's Emily Michelle — she's the one I named my rat after. Daddy and Elizabeth adopted her.

She's two years old and comes from a faraway country called Vietnam. Last but not least, there's Nannie, who's Elizabeth's mother, which makes her my step-grandmother. She helps take care of all of us. Oh, I almost forgot — there are also two pets: Shannon, David Michael's puppy, and Boo-Boo, Daddy's fat, mean cat.

Andrew and I have everything we need at each house. We have toys at each house. We have bicycles at each house. We have clothes and friends and mummies and daddies and stuffed animals at each house. We have two of everything, which is why we are two-twos.

Being a two-two might sound like fun, and it can be. But there's one thing I don't like about being a two-two: I never get to see everybody in my *whole* family at once. I either see the little-house family or the big-house family. So what I had decided I wanted for my birthday was to invite all the people at the little house and all the people at the big house to one party. I just wanted us to be together.

That was why I didn't sound so happy when Daddy asked if I wanted to take some of my friends to the Happy-Time Circus. It meant that once again Daddy was planning one party and Mummy was planning another.

And that was not what I wanted.

3

"Somebody Come And Get Me!"

Becoming seven must make you awfully grown up. Last year, when I was six, all I wanted was parties and presents. I wanted the magician and the pony rides that Daddy said he would get, and I wanted the special birthday meal at McDonalds that Mummy offered me. And I wanted dolls and a bike and new jeans and a stuffed tortoise and an awful lot of other things. But this year all I wanted was my two families to be together — as if we were really one family.

Lately, Mummy and Daddy don't seem

to talk to each other much, even though they both live here in Stoneybrook. You'd think they would phone each other more often.

If they did, maybe we wouldn't have problems like the one we had two weeks ago. It was a Friday. Every other Friday, just before dinner, Mummy drives Andrew and me to the big house for the weekend. On that Friday, my class had been on a field trip. A bus had driven us all the way to Stamford to go to a museum. By the time we came back, it was very late. School had finished and all the children and teachers had gone home. But our mummies and daddies were waiting to pick us up.

Except for mine.

Mummy wasn't waiting and neither was Daddy. No one was there for me. At last, only my teacher, Miss Colman, and I were standing in the school car park.

"Who's supposed to pick you up?" Miss Colman asked. She held my hand so I wouldn't feel so upset.

13

"I'm not sure," I replied.

"Well, let's go inside and I'll phone your parents."

Miss Colman led me into our dark, empty school. I wanted to cry out, "Somebody come and get me!" but I didn't. I didn't have to. Miss Colman talked to my parents. It turned out that Mummy thought Daddy was going to pick me up since I was going to his house for the weekend anyway. And

Daddy thought Mummy was going to pick me up since she had to bring Andrew over to the big house anyway.

It felt as though nobody cared about me. My feelings were very hurt. And that was why I wanted my two families to be more like one family.

I was sitting on my bed, holding Emily Junior, when Mummy came into my room. She was smiling.

"Darling," she said, "I've been thinking. Your birthday is coming up, and seven is a pretty grown-up age."

"Yes, I know," I said, grinning. Had Mummy guessed what I wanted to do?

"So, how would you like to have a posh dinner right here at home? Just you and Andrew and Seth and me. We'll eat in the dining room, we'll use our best china, we'll even have candles. A formal, grown-up supper."

I couldn't believe it! "No!" I howled. I started to cry. "I don't want just us. I want Daddy and my other family, too."

Mummy looked thoughtful. Finally she said, "Karen, I don't think that's a very good idea. For one thing, we can't fit that many people around our table."

"Then Daddy will take us all to the circus," I said. "He could pay for the tickets. I know he could." And that way, I thought, my two families could be together. Also, we would have fun!

But Mummy looked very hurt. "I'm sorry," she said. "I'm sorry I can't afford to give you as big a party as your father can. We'll talk about your birthday another time."

Then she left the room.

I started to cry again.

4

Karen's Big Ideas

Mummy and I had our argument on a Thursday. The next day was a going-to-Daddy's Friday. After school, Andrew and I packed our bags. We never have to take much over to Daddy's since we are two-twos.

While I was packing, Mummy came into my room. I knew she wasn't angry with me. She never stays angry for long.

"Karen," she began, "about your birthday —"

I know I'm not supposed to interrupt people, especially grown-ups, but I did anyway. "Mummy," I said, "don't worry

17

about it. Let's not talk about my birthday now. We can talk on Sunday night when Andrew and I come home. I need to think about some things." The truth was that I was getting a big idea, but I wanted to talk to Daddy about it first.

"Okay," said Mummy, and she gave me a kiss.

"You won't forget to take care of Emily Junior while I'm away, will you?" I asked.

"Of course not. Seth and I know just what to feed her."

"Will you play with her every day, too? She needs exercise."

Mummy paused. "Well . . . Seth will play with her." Mummy doesn't really like rats. So she had been *very* nice when she'd said I could get one.

"That will be great," I told her. "Thank you."

An hour later, Mummy was dropping Andrew and me off at the big house.

"Bye!" we called to her.

"See you Sunday, alligators," she replied. Mummy is so silly.

The door to the big house opened before Andrew and I had even reached the front porch. There was Kristy! Behind her were Daddy and Elizabeth and Emily Michelle and David Michael and Sam and Charlie and Nannie.

Andrew and I ran to them and started hugging everybody.

Nannie said, "I'm so glad to see you!"

Daddy said, "I love you!"

And Emily Michelle said, "Hi, *hi*, HI!" (She doesn't talk much yet.)

Sometimes, evenings at the big house are quiet because all the grown-ups go out and Kristy babysits for us kids. But that night, everyone was at home. We sat round the table in the dining room which is huge. The table is big too so lots of people can fit round it.

"You know what?" I said while we were eating dinner. "It is so, so nice to have two families. I love everyone very much."

"Oh, yuck," replied David Michael.

He is a pain in the neck.

I ignored him. "Daddy," I said, "I've been thinking about my birthday. You know what I want to do? Since I love everyone in my families so much, I want all of us — Mummy and Seth, too — to go to the circus instead of me and my friends."

Daddy opened his mouth, but I rushed on. "And then," I said, "we could come home and have a big, um, formal dinner. Mummy could cook it, but we would eat it here, where everyone can fit." There, I thought. That ought to make Mummy and Daddy *both* happy. We could go to the circus for Daddy, *and* have Mummy's special dinner. And my two families would be together.

But nobody liked the idea. Daddy said, "I think your mother and Seth want to give you a party of their own."

And David Michael said, "Greedy-greedy-greedy-guts!"

And Sam, who likes to tease, said, "Is there anything *else* you want, Karen?

A horse? A swimming pool? A new house?"

I looked at Kristy. She was frowning at me.

What had I done wrong? I was just trying to make everyone happy.

5

Hannie's Wedding

On Saturday morning I was feeling angry with the people in the big house. No one had liked my birthday idea. Sam had teased me, Kristy had frowned at me, and David Michael had called me "greedy-guts".

I decided I didn't want to play with any of those people. I wanted to play with someone nice instead. So I phoned Hannie Papadakis. Hannie is my big-house best friend and she lives over the road from Daddy's. I have a little-house best friend, too. Her name is Nancy Dawes and *she* lives next door to Mummy. Hannie and Nancy and I are all in Miss Colman's class at school.

"Hannie?" I said when I rang her that morning. "It's me, Karen."

"Hi, Karen!" replied Hannie. She sounded very excited. "Where are you? At your mum's house or your dad's house?"

"I'm at Daddy's," I told her.

"Oh, goody. Can I come over?"

"Yes. That's why I was ringing. To invite you over."

"Okay. I'll be there in a minute. I have some important news."

I put the phone down and sat on our front porch and waited. Shannon sat with me and I felt very happy because Shannon is David Michael's puppy and she's usually with him. Or else she's asleep.

I watched Hannie's house. Soon the front door opened and she ran out. She ran all the way to the road. When she reached the pavement, she stopped to check for cars. Then she ran to our steps.

"Hi, Karen," she said. "Guess what. I am going to get married!"

"You are?!" I exclaimed.

"Yes," Hannie replied. She was too excited to sit down. She danced around in front of me.

"Who are you going to marry?" I asked her.

"Scott Hsu. You know. That new boy down the street. Yesterday afternoon I decided I'm in love with him."

"Wow," I said. I didn't know anybody else our age who was in love and going to get married. "When will the wedding be?" I asked.

"I'm not sure. I haven't told Scott about it yet. He doesn't know me. But I have decided what I'm going to wear — Mummy's wedding dress."

"Your mother still has her wedding dress?" I said.

Hannie nodded.

Suddenly I jumped up. "You know what?" I said. "If your mother has her wedding dress, I bet my mother has hers, too. And if she does . . . maybe she and Daddy could get married again! Then Mummy and Daddy and Andrew and I could have our old family back. Just like before the divorce."

"Yes . . . " replied Hannie slowly.

"But first," I went on, "I've got to get Mummy and Daddy together again. They hardly even talk to each other any more. We have to think of some ways to get them to talk on the phone. That would be a start.

After that, they'll see each other a few times, and then they'll decide to get married again."

"Maybe Scott and I could get married when they do."

"Oh, my gosh!" I cried. "That would be perfect! A double wedding! Hannie, we have plans to make."

Hannie and I planned ways to get Mummy and Daddy together. Then we planned the two weddings. It was an exciting morning.

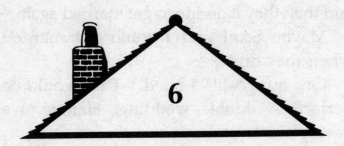

Karen's Birthday List

Hannie and I had some very good ideas that morning. Hannie was going to introduce herself to Scott as soon as possible. She was going to go over to his house and say, "Hi. My name is Hannie Papadakis. I live down the road. Do you want to be friends?" Then she was going to try to play with Scott every day after school. When they knew each other pretty well, she was going to say, "Let's get married. I've got a wedding dress. Do you have a suit?"

I was going to take pictures at the big double wedding.

Hannie and I had some ideas for Mummy and Daddy, too.

"First," I said, "they have to talk to each other more often. Do you know what always makes them talk?"

"What?" asked Hannie.

"A problem. Like when I needed glasses." (I have to wear glasses. I have one pair for reading and writing, and another pair for the rest of the time.) "Or when Andrew had all those bad dreams. Or when Daddy wanted to take Andrew and me on a trip to Washington, D.C., and Mummy didn't want us to go."

"So you need to think of a problem?" said Hannie.

"I already have one," I said. "My birthday. It isn't even here yet, and Mummy and Daddy and *everyone* are angry with me." I told Hannie what was happening with my parties. "David Michael called me 'greedy-guts'," I added. "I bet if I looked *really* greedy, Daddy and Mummy would have a phone call about me."

"What do you mean?" asked Hannie.

"I haven't written my birthday lists," I told her. "Each year, I make two lists, one for Mummy and one for Daddy. This year, I will make one list and I'll give it to Daddy today. It will be so long that I will look like a *real* greedy-guts, and I bet Daddy will telephone Mummy."

"You don't want your parents to be angry with you, do you?" asked Hannie.

"Not really," I replied. "But if it will help them to get married again, then I don't care. I will stop being greedy straight after the wedding."

"The *double* wedding," Hannie corrected me.

"The double wedding," I repeated.

Hannie and I didn't spend the afternoon together. We were too busy. Hannie had to introduce herself to Scott and see if he wanted to play, and I had some work to do in my room.

I closed the door and sat down at my table. On the table were some pieces of paper and some pencils. I pulled a piece of paper in front of me. On the top I wrote: KAREN'S BIRTHDAY LIST. First I wrote down the things I really did want: a stuffed ostrich, a tartan bow for my hair, a doll, a go-cart, and all the books by Roald Dahl, especially the one called *Matilda*. Then I tried to think of some other things for my list. I didn't really want anything else, but I added a new dress, a toy for Emily Junior, pink knee socks, and a pencil box.

The list wasn't nearly long enough, so I wrote down the title of every good book that I'd taken out of the library. It *still* wasn't long enough, so finally I had to go and find a big catalogue. I brought it into my room and I turned to the toy section. There I found page after page of games and toys. I copied down their names, even though I hadn't heard of most of them.

KAREN'S BIRTHDAY
— LIST —
① stuffed ostrich
② plaid bow for hair
③ Little Miss Gorgonzola doll
④ go-cart
⑤ Matilda by Roald Dahl
⑥ _____
⑦ _____ toy
⑧ _____ book PTO
⑨ _____

KBL 2

KBL 3   DRE ...

KBL 4

When I had finished, I had used up four
sheets of paper, front and back. I had listed
two hundred and twelve gifts. I gave the list
to Daddy.

His mouth dropped open.

He rang Mummy that night.

But the next day he didn't say anything
about getting married. He just looked cross.

7

Karen's Accident

"Your turn, Hannie!" called Nancy Dawes.

Hannie threw her stone. It landed on the third square. Hop, hop, hop, hop *over*, land on two feet, hop . . . .

It was break time at school on the Wednesday after I gave Daddy my birthday list. Hannie and Nancy and I were playing hopscotch.

Hannie finished her turn. I was next. I threw my special hopscotch stone. The stone is so special that I keep it in my desk and only use it for hopscotch.

Just as I threw my stone, Hannie said, "I've played with Scott three times now."

"What?" I replied. I tried to turn around while I was hopping — and I slipped on some gravel and fell.

"Ow! Ow!" I cried. I clutched my knee. When I took my hand away, there was blood on it. There was blood all over my knee, too, and I had torn a big hole in my tights.

"Miss Colman! Miss Colman!" Nancy cried.

Our teacher came running. So did nearly all the children in the playground. They crowded around me. My knee hurt an awful lot, but I *did* like getting all the attention. Everyone was saying, "Are you okay, Karen?" Or, "What happened?" Or, "How much does it hurt?"

I felt very special.

Miss Colman helped me inside and down the hall to the nurse's room. The nurse took a look at my knee and then she washed it.

"Hmm," she said. "I think there's some gravel in your knee. I'd like you to see your doctor. Where can I call your mother?"

"At work," I told her. (Mummy works on the mornings that Andrew goes to nursery school.) I gave the nurse Mummy's number. Then the nurse helped me to lie down on a bed.

When the nurse left me alone, I looked around the room. The first thing I saw was . . . a telephone. Suddenly I had an idea. I hobbled over to the phone, picked up the receiver and dialled a number.

"Hello, Daddy?" I said. "It's me, Karen." I made my voice sound tearful and sniffly. "Guess what. I fell over in the playground and there's gravel in my knee and the nurse says a doctor should look at it."

Daddy didn't even ask any questions. "I'll be there straight away," was all he said.

Mummy and Daddy arrived at the nurse's room at almost the same time.

"What are you doing here?" they both asked, as Daddy walked into the room.

Then they both answered, "I got a call to come and get Karen."

I almost giggled. But Mummy and Daddy looked very stern.

"Who called you?" Daddy asked Mummy.

"The nurse," she replied. "Who called you?"

"Karen," Daddy replied.

My parents looked at me. "Well?" they said.

"I – I just needed you," I told them. "I needed both of you."

Why did my parents look so angry?

"Karen," said Mummy, "when you're living with me, then you rely on me. You only call Daddy in an *emergency*. Do you understand?"

I nodded. I tried not to cry. But I felt better as Daddy carried me to Mummy's car. He and Mummy talked the whole way home. They were talking about me and what I'd done and the birthday list. They didn't sound too happy with me. But that was okay. At least they were talking.

They even called "Goodbye!" to each other as Daddy left for work, and Mummy and I left for the doctor's surgery.

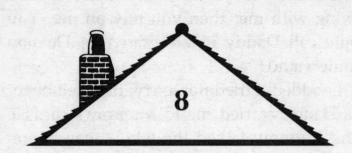

8

Old Pictures

The doctor did find some gravel in my knee. It hurt a lot when she took it out, and I yelled, "Ow! Stop it!" But then she put a *big* bandage on my knee and even gave me a piece of butterscotch. I liked the bandage very, very much and I liked the butterscotch too.

By Saturday, my knee was so much better that I didn't even need the bandage any more. I took it off and let everyone see my wound. Most people said, "Er! Yuk!" but Andrew said "Great!"

Saturday was a rainy day. I didn't feel like going outside, so I decided to work on one of the plans Hannie and I had made. Mummy and Daddy hadn't spoken to each other since they came to school when I hurt my knee. It was time for them to start thinking about their wedding. So I went up to the attic in the little house. I was looking for two things — Mummy's wedding dress, and an album of the pictures that had been taken at their wedding. I'd never seen the album, but Hannie said her parents had one. She said they kept it out on the coffee table in their living room. Hannie had been looking at it a lot lately to see how her wedding with Scott should go.

She had already decided what she and Scott would need: the wedding dress, Scott's suit, a cake, flowers, a flower girl, two bridesmaids, two ushers, a photographer (that would be me), a vicar, and guests. I thought that sounded like an awful lot.

I climbed the stairs to our attic. I turned

on the light. The attic was cold, so I had to go back to my room to get a sweater. Then I returned to the attic.

I love attics — you never know what you'll find in them. I looked around ours. I hadn't been there for a long time. The first thing I saw was my old tricycle. I rode it around. Then I found a box full of baby toys. I poked through them. Why was Mummy saving them? Next I found Eugene. Eugene was a gigantic doll my grandparents had given me. I had never liked Eugene much so I sat him in a corner.

Okay. It was time to find the wedding album and Mummy's dress. The album was easy to find, it was sitting on a shelf. But I couldn't find the dress. I looked and looked. Finally I decided I was wasting time.

I forgot about the dress. Instead I took the album downstairs. I sat on the living room sofa and flipped through it. When I came to the pages that showed Mummy and Daddy kissing each other and laughing and eating

wedding cake, I put the book on the coffee table. I left it open. Then I left the room.

Five minutes later I heard Seth exclaim, "Lisa! What *is* this?"

(Lisa is Mummy.)

"What?" cried Mummy. She ran into the living room.

"*This*," said Seth. He sounded angry.

I peeped into the living room. I watched Mummy and Seth.

"I'm sorry," said Mummy. "I don't know

41

how it got there. But *I* didn't — " Mummy looked up then and saw me. "Karen?" she said. "Do you know anything about this?"

"Well, I —" I began. "I put it there."

"The pictures of Daddy's and my wedding? *Why?*" asked Mummy.

"I don't know," I said. I had thought Mummy would be able to work it out. Didn't she see that she and *Daddy* should be married?

"Young lady," said Mummy. (She only says that when she is *very*, *very* angry.) "If I were you, I would remember that your birthday is around the corner. I don't understand some of the things you've been doing recently. I think you'd better watch it!"

I nodded. Then I went to my room. I didn't understand Mummy, either. What did my birthday have to do with anything? And why couldn't she and Daddy see that they should be married again?

Parents are very confusing. They are unfair, too.

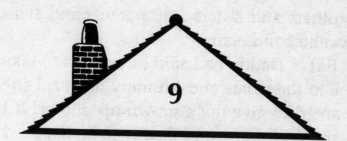

The Biggest
Birthday Party Ever

I didn't know what to do. I took Emily Junior out of her cage and played with her for a while. I like to watch her nose. When she twitches it, her whiskers twitch, too. Emily Junior is always sniffing, sniffing, sniffing.

While Emily Junior sniffed around my room, I thought about Mummy and Daddy; I thought about Seth and Elizabeth; and I thought about my birthday. I just had to get my two families together. That way Mummy and Daddy would have to talk to each other.

43

And I could spend the day with all my brothers and sisters, my parents and step-parents, and Nannie.

But — Daddy had said he wanted to take me to the circus and Mummy had said she wanted to give me a grown-up dinner. If I wanted Mummy and Daddy to be happy, I would have to go ahead with my plans for a *huge* birthday — the circus and a dinner with both my families. I didn't care if I looked like a greedy-guts. After all, it was *my* birthday, wasn't it?

There was only one thing to do. I would have to plan my own party.

I sat down at my desk. I found some paper and crayons. On one piece of paper, I wrote:

COME TO THE BIGGEST BIRTHDAY PARTY EVER!
SEE THE CIRCUS! HAVE A SPECIAL DINNER
(at Daddy's)!
BRING YOUR PRESENTS!
KAREN IS TURNING SEVEN!

Then I wrote down the date of the party and the time it would start. I said we should meet at the circus. I even drew a picture of a clown.

When I had finished, I decided the invitation looked very nice. So I made lots more until there were enough for Mummy, Seth, Andrew, Daddy, Elizabeth, Kristy, Sam, Charlie, David Michael, Emily Michelle, and Nannie. I wanted to invite Hannie and Nancy, but I decided not to. This was just a party for my two families.

I put the invitations in envelopes. Then I addressed them and stuck stamps on them.

My invitations were ready to go. All I had to do was walk down the street and drop them in the letterbox. So I put Emily Junior back in her cage and left my room. As I passed Andrew's room, I noticed that his door was closed and he had hung a sign on the knob. It said DO NOT DISTURB. Andrew had been in his room a lot lately with that sign up.

I wondered what he was doing.

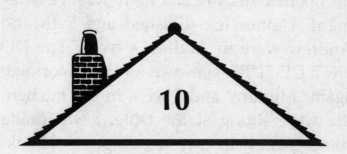

10

Trouble!

Uh-oh.

I was in trouble. At least I was pretty sure I was. Nobody had punished me, but nobody was very happy with me, either.

It started when Daddy and the people at the big house got their invitations to my birthday. Even though I had sent all the invitations at the same time, the little-house invitations had not arrived yet.

You know the post.

Anyway, Daddy spoiled my surprise. He spoiled it by phoning Mummy as soon as he opened his invitation. It was Tuesday night. Dinner had finished and Seth and Andrew were in Andrew's room. The DO NOT DISTURB sign was on the doorknob again. Mummy and I were in the kitchen. We were sitting at the table. I was doing some pages in my reading workbook. Mummy was paying bills.

When the phone rang, I let Mummy answer it. Usually I yell, "I'll get it!" But Mummy was right next to the phone. Besides, I had almost finished the page about vowel sounds. As soon as I finished it, I had only one more page to go. Then my homework would be done.

"Hello?" said Mummy. She paused. Then she said. "Oh, hi!" She put her hand over the receiver. "It's Daddy," she told me.

I grinned. Good! Mummy and Daddy were talking on the phone. Maybe Mummy had been thinking about their wedding pictures and they would get married again soon.

"What?!" exclaimed Mummy. "She did *what*?"

48

I stopped daydreaming. Mummy sounded angry.

"I can't believe she did that," said Mummy. "You *all* received invitations? . . . No, we haven't got any." Mummy looked *very* crossly at me. Then her cross look changed to a different kind of look. "Ex*cuse* me?" she said. "Bringing up a *brat*? I'm not the only one bringing up Karen and Andrew. You're bringing them up too, you know. Hold on just a minute." Mummy looked at me again. "Karen, would you please leave the room?" she said.

"But I haven't finished my homework," I replied.

"*Karen*."

"Okay, okay."

I left the kitchen and went to the dining room. Mummy hadn't said how *far* I had to go. I listened to the rest of her conversation and heard her and Daddy having an argument. And it was all about me. I could tell by the things I heard Mummy say. They were very angry: they said I was greedy;

they said I was spoilt; and they blamed each other.

What had gone wrong? I hadn't meant to make Mummy and Daddy have a row.

The next day the little-house invitations arrived. Mummy phoned Daddy and they had another argument. I listened to Mummy's end of the row from under the table in the dining room. As soon as Mummy had finished yelling at Daddy, she phoned a friend of hers.

"Pam?" she said. "I'm worried about Karen." Mummy told Pam everything. She told her about my birthday list. She told her about the invitations and the wedding album and phoning Daddy when I hurt my knee. "I thought Karen had adjusted to the divorce and to Seth," Mummy said to Pam. "But now I don't know. I don't know at all. And her father and I are blaming each other."

I crawled out from under the table. I went into the living room. No one was there, so I sat down in a chair and thought. All I wanted was for my two families to be together on my birthday . . . and for Mummy and Daddy to get married again. But no one seemed to understand.

Sometimes it isn't easy being six. Or having parents who are divorced.

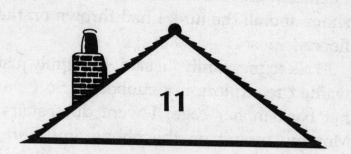

A Talk With Kristy

I wandered upstairs to my bedroom. I passed the DO NOT DISTURB sign again. I still didn't know what Andrew and Seth were doing.

When I got to my room, I took Emily Junior out of her cage and put her on the floor.

Sniff, sniff, sniff. Twitch, twitch, twitch.

"I wish you could talk," I said to Emily. "If you were Nicodemus from *Mrs Frisby and the Rats of NIMH*, I bet you'd talk to me."

Emily poked her nose into my cupboard.

Then she crept inside. She sniffed at my shoes and all the junk I had thrown on the floor.

"Talk to me, Emily," I said. But Emily just wanted to explore my cupboard. So I put her back in her cage. I went downstairs. Mummy wasn't on the phone any more, she was in the living room.

"Mummy," I said, "I need to make a phone call. And I would like some privacy, please, so I'm going to close the door to the kitchen."

Mummy looked surprised. "All right," she said.

I closed myself into the kitchen. I dialled the number of the big house.

A voice answered the phone. It said, "Brewer and Thomas Summer Home. Some are home, some are not."

I knew it was Sam. He is always joking and playing tricks.

"Very funny, Sam," I said. "This is Karen."

"Karen? Karen who?"

"Karen *Brewer*. Your sister. Can I please talk to Kristy?"

"I don't know. Can you?"

"Sa-am. *Please*?"

"Okay. Here she is."

"Hi," I said, when Kristy got on the phone. "It's me, Karen. Your sister," I added, just in case. "I need to talk to you." Kristy and I usually talk twice a week when I'm at the little house.

"What's up?" asked Kristy.

"Mummy and Daddy are angry with me," I told her.

"I'm not surprised," said Kristy. "You should have seen your father's face when we got the invitations yesterday. He's upset about the party."

"But I thought the party was a good idea."

"Karen, I have never seen anyone who wanted as much for one birthday as you do. The circus, the dinner — and two hundred and twelve presents. Everyone is so cross you'll be lucky if you get *any* presents at all.

I can't believe you actually put 'Bring your presents' on the invitations. That's so rude."

Maybe I shouldn't have added that line. But . . . .

How could I explain to Kristy what I *really* wanted? It's hard to talk to someone who's cross with you.

What I wanted didn't have anything to do with presents. I just wanted to see my families together on my birthday. And then, of course, I wanted the wedding. But that could wait.

"Oh, Kristy, you don't understand anything!" I cried. Then I hung up the phone without saying goodbye. I felt worse than ever.

I marched into the living room. "GOODNIGHT!" I yelled at Mummy.

I marched upstairs. "GOODNIGHT!" I yelled to Andrew and Seth.

I marched into my room. I closed my door. I put on my nightdress and got into bed. But I couldn't fall asleep. I could hear

Emily Junior rustling around in her cage. I don't think she could sleep, either.

So I sang the saddest song I knew in the saddest voice I could make. I sang it over and over again until Emily Junior and I were both asleep.

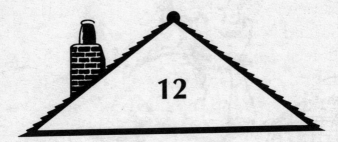

Scott Dumps Hannie

Usually I like going-to-Daddy's weekends. But not this time.

Everyone thought I was a greedy-guts. So I was very cross with them. They didn't understand anything.

On Saturday I rang Hannie. Her mother answered the phone.

"Hannie isn't here," said Mrs Papadakis. "She's at Scott Hsu's. Why don't you go over there? I'm sure Hannie and Scott would be glad to see you."

At least *some*one would be glad to see me, I thought.

"Thank you," I told Mrs Papadakis.

I decided to leave straight away. "I'm going to Scott Hsu's!" I yelled as I left the house, but I don't think anyone cared.

I had never met Scott, but Hannie had pointed out his house to me several times. "That's where *he* lives," she would say. Then she would sigh deeply.

"How does it feel to be in love?" I would ask her.

"It feels . . . wonderful."

I was halfway to Scott's house when I saw someone coming towards me. The person got closer and closer.

It was Hannie.

"Hannie!" I cried. "Hi! I'm here for the weekend."

Hannie didn't answer me. She looked upset.

"What's wrong?" I asked.

"Scott doesn't want to marry me."

"Doesn't he?"

Hannie shook her head. "No. We were such good friends, too. We were playing together almost every day. I gave Scott some sweets once, and he gave me a caterpillar. Then today I told him I was thinking about weddings. I told him about my mother's dress and about flowers and everything."

"Did you tell him about double weddings?" I asked.

"Yes." Hannie nodded. I had turned around and we were walking back to our houses.

"Then," Hannie went on, "I said, 'Scott, we're such good friends now, I think we should get married.' And he said, 'Are you kidding?' And I said, 'No.' And he said, 'We aren't old enough to get married.' And I said, 'But I'm in love with you.' And you know what Scott did?"

I shook my head. "No. What?" I was fascinated.

"He said, 'Yuk!!' And then his brother started singing, 'Hannie and Scott, sitting in a tree. K-I-S-S-I-N-G'."

"First comes love," I continued, "then comes marriage —"

"Karen, you don't have to finish the song," said Hannie. "I know it myself, thank you."

Gosh! *Everyone* was in a bad mood today.

"Then what happened?" I asked.

"Then Scott and his brother ran round to their back garden and I left."

"You left?" I repeated. "Without finding out if Scott loves you?"

"He doesn't love me," said Hannie.

"But he gave you a caterpillar."

"Friends give each other things sometimes. It doesn't mean they are in love."

"Oh." I kicked a pebble.

"Let's face it," said Hannie. "Scott dumped me."

Hannie was the first person I knew who had been dumped.

We reached Hannie's house. "I'm going to go and lie down for a while," she said.

"Okay." I watched Hannie walk across her front garden. "Sorry the wedding is off!" I called after her.

That was awful. Now when Mummy and Daddy got married again, they couldn't have a double wedding.

13

Help From Nannie

Usually David Michael calls me either "Karen" or "Professor". He calls me "Professor" because of my glasses. It's a nice nickname, not a nasty one. But on Saturday he didn't call me anything except "greedy-guts". He called me that so many times that Nannie told him to stop it.

I smiled at Nannie. Nannie hadn't said a word to me about my birthday or my invitations or the list of two hundred and twelve presents. She hadn't called me names like David Michael had. She hadn't frowned at me like Kristy had.

Maybe Nannie wasn't angry with me. Maybe I could talk to her about my birthday. I decided it would be safe to try.

After supper on Saturday, I found Nannie in the study. The TV was on, but Nannie wasn't looking at it because she was looking at her knitting.

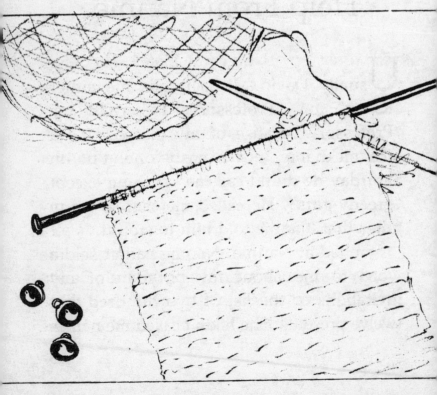

"Hi," I said. I settled myself on the sofa next to Nannie. "What are you making?"

"A sweater for Emily," Nannie replied. "Do you think she'll like it?"

I nodded. "Nannie?"

"Yes?"

"I think people are angry with me about my birthday."

"Do you?"

"Yes."

Nannie didn't sound angry, and she wasn't accusing me of anything. Maybe I could tell her about my families — she might understand.

"You know why I sent out the invitations?" I said.

"No. Why?" replied Nannie. She put her knitting down and looked at me.

"I want my two families together on my birthday this year," I told her. "That's all I *really* want. Not parties or presents or the circus or anything. Mummy and Daddy always seem angry with each other these days. Either they don't talk, or they have arguments over the phone. And I don't want that. I want Mummy and Daddy and Seth and Elizabeth and you and my brothers and sisters — all of them — together."

"Oh, Karen." Nannie put her arm around me. "Your mummy and daddy aren't angry with each other. Just a little cross. And they're very busy. They both have their own families now. Also we have Emily Michelle, and your mummy has her job. Even if that weren't true, though, I'm not sure that bringing your two families together would be a good idea. They are two families for a reason. Seth and Elizabeth would feel uncomfortable with each other. No, it's just not a good idea. And it isn't going to happen, Karen. I'm sorry, but it isn't."

I nodded. Maybe deep down I had known all along that it wouldn't happen. "What should I do now?" I asked Nannie.

"Well, if you can't have your two families together for your birthday, what do you want instead?"

"Mummy's party at home, and Daddy's circus party. Just what they suggested."

"Okay. And how about presents?"

"I don't really want two hundred and twelve. I just made up that list because I knew Daddy would phone Mummy and then they'd have to talk to each other. I only want the first five things on the list."

"Okay," said Nannie. "I'll tell your father for you. But I won't tell him why you made the long list."

"Thank you, Nannie." I kissed her goodnight. Then I went upstairs to bed.

I fell asleep thinking that I used to feel lucky to be a two-two. Now I wished I were a one-one.

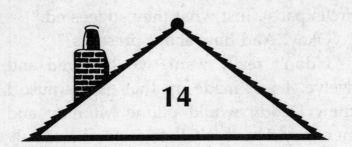

14

Help From Seth

On Sunday night, Andrew and I went back to the little house. Nannie had told Daddy about my birthday plans, but it was up to me to tell Mummy.

I decided to talk to Seth first. Seth was like Nannie. He hadn't said anything to me about my birthday and he didn't seem cross or upset.

I caught Seth just as he was about to go into Andrew's room. Andrew was putting out the DO NOT DISTURB sign.

"Seth?" I said. "Can I talk to you for a minute?"

"Of course," replied Seth. He turned to Andrew. "I'll be right in. Just let me talk to Karen first."

Seth and I sat on my bed.

"Seth?" I said. "I know Mummy is angry about my birthday, so I've been thinking. I decided I do want a party here after all. The grown-up kind that she was talking about.

And I only want the first five things on that list, especially the books. That's all." (I couldn't tell Seth about the two families. I decided that would be between Nannie and me.)

"I think your mother will be happy to hear that," Seth said. He gave me a kiss. Then he called Mummy into my room and I told her my news.

Mummy was very happy. "Who do you want to invite?" she asked.

"Just us, like you said. You and Seth and Andrew and me . . . and Emily Junior?"

"I'm not sure a rat would be a good party guest," said Mummy. "Emily Junior doesn't know how to sit still."

I nodded. "Okay. No Emily."

"How about decorations?" asked Mummy.

"Balloons and crêpe paper," I said. I was beginning to feel a little excited. "A big bunch of balloons over my place at the table."

"And food? You can have anything you want."

That was easy. "Hamburgers, mashed potatoes, cake, and ice cream," I said.

"Terrific," Mummy replied. "Vanilla or chocolate cake?"

"Chocolate. And strawberry ice cream."

"Seth!" Andrew called just then. "Come and help me with Karen's — I mean, come and help me!"

Seth grinned. "I'd better go. Andrew and I are working on an important project."

Seth left Mummy and me alone. "I'm so glad you changed your mind, Karen," said Mummy. "I think you are really growing up."

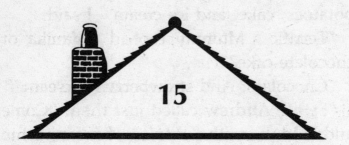

15

Curious Karen

"**O**nly two more days until my birthday! Only two more days until my birthday!" I sang.

I could hardly wait. It seemed like forever since my sixth birthday. And now that I'd decided to have the parties that Mummy and Daddy wanted, I felt better. I had wanted my two families together — but not if everyone was going to be angry.

It was Thursday and school had finished. "Just think," I said to Andrew. "In two days you'll be going to the Happy-Time Circus. What are you going to wear?"

"Wear?" Andrew repeated. "Clothes."

"Anything special?"

"I don't know." Andrew was busy with his cars and trucks.

I couldn't believe he hadn't planned his circus outfit. I had planned my circus outfit, the outfit for Mummy's posh party, and the outfit for my class party at school. This is what I was going to wear:

School party: baggy shirt, red-and-white-striped skirt

Mummy's party: posh yellow dress, ribbons in my hair

Circus party: blue jeans, unicorn sweatshirt

Daddy and I had sent out invitations for the circus party. We had found ones with clowns and balloons on them. I had invited Andrew, everyone in the big-house family, Hannie, Nancy, Scott Hsu (he was Hannie's idea; she wanted to be friends with him again), and three other children. The circus was going to be great fun.

I was so excited that I was getting ants in my pants. That's what my big brother Sam would say. How, I wondered, could I wait until my first party the next day? How could I wait until the next night to open some presents? I couldn't. That was all there was to it.

"Andrew?" I said. "Where's Mummy?"

"Next door with Nancy's mummy," he replied. "Vroom, vroom." Andrew never even looked up from his cars and trucks.

Well, this was perfect. It was time to do a little present-hunting. I did that before my last birthday, and just before Christmas, too.

The first place I looked was under Mummy and Seth's bed. Nothing.

Then I looked in Seth's cupboard. Yes! On the floor was a present. The card read, "For Karen, from Seth. Happy birthday, seven-year-old!" Okay. Now I had to be very careful. Sneaking a look at presents is not easy. Often, adults can work out that you've done it. But I am an expert.

I slid the ribbon off to one side without untying it. Then I peeled back a piece of tape — very, very carefully. The end of the parcel came undone. I looked inside. A book! I peeled away some more tape. The book was *Matilda*, by Roald Dahl! Then, just as carefully, I put the paper back where it had been, stuck the tape down again, and

slid the ribbon on. Pretty good. I didn't think anyone would ever know the present had been peeped at.

Before Mummy came home, I found and opened the rest of my presents — except for Andrew's. He must have hidden it very well. I did find a box under his bed that said LOOK IN HERE in Seth's handwriting, but I didn't look. I knew it was a trick.

Anyway, Mummy was giving me the stuffed ostrich, the tartan bow for my hair, and some clothes. Goody! Now I really couldn't wait until the next night.

Having birthdays is so much fun. When I was seven, David Michael and I would be the same age at last. And I would be the same age as the other children in my class. (I am the youngest, since I skipped a grade.)

"Oh, tomorrow, tomorrow," I sang. "Please hurry up and get here!"

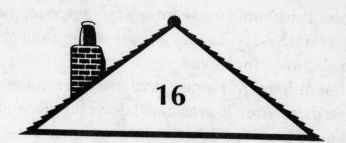

16

The School Party

Tomorrow *finally* came. Now it was today. It was the day of Mummy's party, and it was the day of my party in Miss Colman's class!

Just as I had planned, I wore my baggy shirt and my red-and-white-striped skirt to school. I tied a red ribbon in my hair. On my feet I wore my party shoes. They are shiny and black. Usually I'm not allowed to wear them to school, but Mummy said that my birthday was a special occasion.

School is over at two-forty-five. On my

birthday, Mummy was going to come at one-thirty and we were going to spend the rest of the day having a party. Mummy was going to bring cakes.

Waiting until one-thirty was very, very hard for me. It was hard for Hannie and Nancy and the other children in my class, too. We were going to play games and eat, and Miss Colman said she had a special treat for us. I bet everyone was very glad it was my birthday.

I know I was.

At one-thirty on the dot, I heard a knock on our classroom door.

"My mum is here!" I cried. "That's her! I know it is! She's got the cakes!"

"Karen, settle down," said Miss Colman gently.

I sat quietly at my desk while Miss Colman opened the door. There stood Mummy with the box of cakes and — *Andrew*. Andrew? What was he doing? He wasn't invited. Little brothers aren't supposed to come to class parties.

Andrew followed Mummy into the room, looking shy. A couple of children nudged each other and pointed at him, but they didn't have a chance to say anything. That was because Miss Colman said, "It's time for the party to begin! The first thing we're going to do is the surprise. We're going to make hats!"

Miss Colman and Mummy helped us to make pointy party hats. We decorated the hats with glitter and feathers. I printed BIRTHDAY GIRL on mine with a special pen that wrote in sparkles. Even Andrew made a hat.

Then Miss Colman said, "Time for refreshments!" We sat at our desks. (Andrew sat with me.) Mummy and Miss Colman gave out paper napkins, cups, party blowers, and the cakes. Horrid Ricky Torres blew his blower in my face. I blew mine back in his face. I started to call him "Yicky Ricky", but just then Mummy stuck a candle in my cake. She lit it and everyone sang "Happy Birthday". Then I blew the candle out.

I love having people sing to me.

We ate the cakes. Yum! Mummy had decorated then to look like cats. I ate my cat's nose first, then the rest of his face, then the rest of the icing, and finally the cake part.

When we had finished eating, we played Pin-the-Tail-on-the-Donkey. Guess who won? Andrew! He won fair and square.

"He's good," said Ricky Torres.

I felt proud of Andrew. "My brother is good at lots of things," I said. I decided I was glad he had come to my party.

When the bell rang, everyone was sorry. Usually we like the end of the week, but not that day. We were having fun.

I had something to look forward to, though — Mummy's party!

17

Mummy's Party

That night, Seth came home early for my party. "I need time to get ready," he said. "This is a formal party, so I have to dress up. Andrew, are you going to dress up, too? I'm going to wear my suit."

Andrew hates wearing his suit, but he didn't want to be the only person at our party who wasn't dressed up, so he said, "Okay."

Everyone went to their rooms to change their clothes. I put on my posh yellow dress, the one with a lot of lace on it. Then I put on my white tights and my black party shoes. Just as I had planned, I tied yellow ribbons in my hair. But first I brushed my hair over and over again to make sure it was shiny and there were no tangles.

When I was dressed I went downstairs. Mummy was waiting in the living room. She was wearing a dress that so far she had only worn to grown-up parties. It is black and has beads on it.

"Mummy, you look so pretty!" I exclaimed.

"Thank you," said Mummy, kissing me. "Happy birthday, Karen."

Andrew and Seth came downstairs in their suits. Andrew was even wearing his bow-tie. (It's not a real bow-tie — if you pull it, it will come off his shirt.)

"Shall we have drinks and nibbles in the living room first?" asked Mummy.

Ooh. Drinks and nibbles. This really was a grown-up party.

Mummy poured ginger ale for each of us. Then she passed around crisps and a plate with carrot sticks, celery sticks, and olives on it. I ate an olive and felt as if I were *much* older than almost seven. I even remembered to put the stone in my napkin where no one could see it.

"Now," said Seth, "it's dinner-time."

Mummy and Seth and Andrew and I walked into the dining room. The lights were off and candles were burning on the table. Mummy was letting us use real china and real silver. A bunch of pink balloons was hanging over my place and in the middle of the table was a bouquet of flowers.

"This is so posh!" I said in a whisper.

We ate hamburgers and mashed potatoes, and Mummy and Seth ate some salad. Then it was time for . . . the birthday cake!

Mummy carried it out of the kitchen.

"Happy birthday to you!" sang my little-house family.

The cake was covered with icing flowers. Andrew and I each got a pink rose. The pink roses matched the strawberry ice cream.

"Well," said Mummy when we were all full, "I think it's time for —"

"Presents?" I asked.

Mummy nodded.

"Hurray! Hurray!" I got out of my chair and began jumping up and down.

"Karen," said Mummy. (I knew she meant "Calm down".)

I opened my presents in the living room. There were the ostrich, the bow, the new clothes, and *Matilda*. I acted very surprised, and no one guessed that I had already peeped at the presents.

Then Andrew said, "Time for *my* present!"

"I'll help you get it," said Seth.

Andrew and Seth went upstairs. They came down carrying the box that said LOOK IN HERE.

"Is your present really in there?" I asked.

"Yes," said Andrew.

Hmm. I would never have guessed.

Inside the box was a playground for Emily Junior. Andrew and Seth had *made* it. That's why Andrew had been hanging the DO NOT DISTURB sign on his door.

"See?" said Andrew. "There's a maze and a tunnel and a seesaw. Now Emily Junior will never get bored."

"Thanks, Andrew," I said. I gave him a hug. I didn't tell anybody, but I liked Andrew's present best of all.

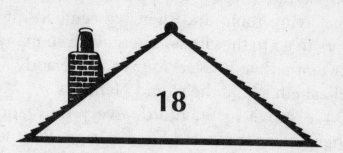

The Circus Party

Later that evening, Mummy and Seth drove Andrew and me to the big house. My little-house party was over. The next day would be . . . circus day!

Saturday was my actual birthday. It was the day I would *really* be seven. When I woke up on Saturday, the sun was shining and the sky was blue. It was perfect birthday weather!

At midday, my friends began arriving at the big house.

"Happy birthday, Karen!" they cried. They

all brought presents. We put the presents in the living room and then we climbed into cars to go to the circus. There were so many of us that we needed four cars — Daddy's, Elizabeth's, Charlie's, and Nannie's.

We drove to Stamford. Every now and then, someone would see a sign for the Happy-Time Circus, and we would cheer.

"We're almost there!" I shouted.

The Happy-Time Circus was an indoor circus, not an outdoor circus under a tent. We drove to a big building and parked the cars in a car park. Then we went inside the building. Daddy reached in his pocket and pulled out an envelope which held the circus tickets. He handed them to a man, and we followed a crowd of people into an arena.

"Ooh," I said softly. "Is this the circus?"

"It's going to be," replied Daddy.

We were standing in one of the hugest places I've ever seen. And we were really high up. Below us, on the floor, were three rings. Above us were the tightropes and trapeze bars. We found our seats, and for a few moments we were quiet.

I noticed that all around us, children were waving fancy torches. Some of them looked like tigers, some like sparkly fairy dust. Daddy bought us each a torch.

"Can we get popcorn?" I asked.

"Or candyfloss?" asked Andrew.

"No food," said Daddy. "Wait until we're home. We'll have a special treat then."

We waited patiently for the circus to start. Hannie was sitting next to me. On her other side was Scott Hsu.

"Are you going to get married?" I asked her.

Hannie shook her head. "Not yet. Scott has to fall in love with me first." Hannie turned to Scott. "Scott?" she said. "Here. You can have my torch, okay?"

"Really?" Scott replied. "Gosh, thanks!" Scott grinned at Hannie.

Hannie grinned at me.

Soon the arena grew dark. We waved our torches around. The ringmaster stepped into the centre ring. "Welcome to the Happy-Time Circus!" he said. "Today you will see the world's most exciting show — clowns and animals, death-defying acts high above your head, jugglers and acrobats and more."

The show began. A cowboy clown chased another cowboy clown round and round the centre ring. They shot at each other with cap guns. (The guns made Emily Michelle cry.) One clown pushed the other onto a piano with a *crash!*

We laughed and laughed.

We watched Paddy's Trained Poodles and Biff's Trained Bears. We saw a parade of elephants. We saw white horses. We saw the Cecily Sisters turn somersaults in the air using the trapeze.

"How do they do that?" I asked Hannie.

She didn't answer. She was watching a woman selling ice cream. "Can we get some ice cream?" she asked Daddy.

"Sorry," said Daddy. "Wait until we're home. We'll have plenty to eat there."

"Boo," whispered Hannie.

"If I had any money," said Scott, "I'd buy you *two* ice creams, Hannie."

Hannie grinned again.

We settled back to watch the rest of the show. I decided I liked the clowns best.

After the Circus

After the circus I went home in Daddy's car. Andrew, Hannie, Scott, and Sam were with us. "Quick!" said Daddy. "Everybody tell me your favourite part of the circus!"

"The clowns," I said.

"Yes, the cowboy clowns," agreed Scott.

"The pretty lady clowns," said Hannie.

"My torch," said Andrew.

"The gorilla," said Sam.

"What gorilla?" I asked.

"Just testing you," said Sam. He is such a tease.

When we reached our house, Nannie showed everyone into the dining room. We sat down at the table. Hannie sat next to Scott. My friends and I put on party hats and waited.

Soon the door to the kitchen opened. In came Daddy. He was carrying a big cake. "Happy birthday to you!" everyone sang. Daddy put the cake in front of me. I counted seven candles and one for luck.

The cake looked like the circus. It was decorated with clowns and acrobats and elephants. Daddy and Nannie served the cake. My piece had a clown face on it!

"Eat up!" said Daddy, so we ate our cake and ice cream.

Then it was time for presents. I sat on the sofa in the living room. The presents were stacked next to me.

"Open mine first!" said Hannie.

So I did. Inside was a stuffed elephant. "To remind you of the circus," said Hannie.

"Thanks!" I exclaimed. "I'll call him Babar."

I opened the rest of the presents. Every
now and then I glanced at Hannie and Scott.
They were always together. When the party
was over, Hannie whispered to me as she
was leaving, "I asked Scott to marry me
again, and this time he said, 'Yes'. I'm so
happy!"

"I'm happy, too," I told her. "I can't wait
for the wedding!"

Hannie was the last guest to leave. When
she had gone, I looked round the living

room at my gifts and the wrapping paper and ribbon.

"Do you want to open your family presents now?" asked Daddy.

"Could I wait until tomorrow?" I replied. "That way I can stretch out my birthday."

"Of course," said Daddy, "but honestly, Karen, I have never seen anyone make such a big thing over her birthday as you."

"Big thing?" I repeated.

"Yes," said Daddy. "Two hundred and twelve presents, a huge party."

"Becoming seven is exciting," I said.

"Maybe," replied Daddy. "But you can celebrate your birthday without being greedy."

So Daddy still thought I was greedy. I knew the time had come to tell him the truth. I would have to say it even if it was very, very hard.

"Daddy," I began, "I didn't really want two hundred and twelve presents. I just knew that if I asked for them you would have to phone Mummy and talk to her. You never talk to each other any more. And I wanted the big party so you and Mummy would be together. Andrew and I like to see you together. We . . . we want you to get married again."

"Oh, Karen," said Daddy. He opened his arms for a hug. "That's not going to happen," he told me. "We're both married to other people now. And we're both happily married."

"I know," I said. I didn't understand *why* it was so. But I knew that that was the way things were.

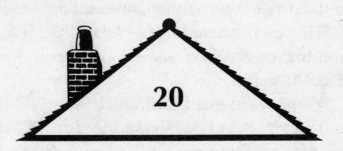

20

The Surprise

Daddy and I talked for a long time that night. I told him I wished that he and Mummy would phone each other just a little more often, and *not* argue so often. I told him again how much Andrew and I missed seeing him and Mummy together. And I told him how awful I felt when he and Mummy "forgot" me at school after the field trip.

Guess what happened then?

Daddy phoned Mummy. And he didn't even

make me leave the kitchen. He let me stay and listen to the phone conversation.

"Hi, Lisa," he said. "It's Watson. . . . No, nothing's wrong. We had a great day. The circus was fun —"

"We saw clowns!" I shouted.

"Did you hear that?" asked Daddy. "That was Karen telling you we saw clowns. And elephants and trained animals and a lot of other things. Anyway, Karen and I have just had a little talk." Daddy told Mummy everything we'd discussed. "So I think," he went on, "that we should make an effort to stay in touch more. After all, Karen and Andrew are still *our* children. Our children *together*, despite the divorce." Mummy must have agreed with Daddy because the next thing Daddy said was, "I'm glad you feel that way. Okay, we'll see you tomorrow."

When Daddy put down the phone I was grinning. I bet my smile was a mile wide. "Thank you!" I cried.

The next day I waited all morning and part of the afternoon to open my family presents. Finally I said, "Okay, I'm ready!"

"Really?" said Sam. "Are you sure you don't want to wait until next year and open them when you're eight?"

"Sa-am!" I cried. "No!"

"Or you could wait until you're twelve. Then you could open six years' worth of presents at once. It would probably take you a whole day."

"No!" I cried. "Now!" But I knew Sam was just teasing again.

Everyone scattered to get the presents they'd been hiding. (I hadn't searched for presents at the big house. There were always too many people around.) When everyone came back, I was sitting next to another pile of presents. Daddy gave me the doll. Elizabeth gave me *Charlie and the Chocolate Factory* and *James and the Giant Peach* by Roald Dahl. Kristy gave me another book by Roald Dahl. It was called *The Witches*.

"A whole book about witches!" I exclaimed.

There were presents from everyone (except Andrew). Even Emily gave me a present. It was a piece of paper with a big brown scribble on it.

"Emmy," she said. "Rat."

It was a picture of Emily Junior.

"Oh, it's beautiful!" I cried. "I'll hang it up in my room here."

Emily smiled. She was very pleased with herself.

But the best surprise was when Mummy and Seth arrived to pick Andrew and me up. They came inside and looked at my presents. They told Emily how nice her picture was, and they listened while I told them about the circus party.

Then Mummy said, "Karen, Daddy and I had a talk. We want you to know we will never 'forget' you again. And from now on we will listen to you more carefully. Is that a deal?"

"It's a deal!" I cried.

I had given up on their wedding. I knew it wouldn't happen. Seth and Elizabeth

were standing right in front of me and they were part of my family. No, my *two* families, I corrected myself. I had *two* families and that wouldn't change.

I thought about my birthday — the parties and cakes and presents and the circus. You know what the best part was? It was right now. It was my two families together, even if it was just for a few minutes.

GREEN WATCH by Anthony Masters

GREEN WATCH is a new series of fast moving environmental thrillers, in which a group of young people battle against the odds to save the natural world from ruthless exploitation. All titles are printed on recycled paper.

BATTLE FOR THE BADGERS
Tim's been sent to stay with his weird Uncle Seb and his two kids, Flower and Brian, who run Green Watch – an environmental pressure group. At first Tim thinks they're a bunch of cranks – but soon he finds himself battling to save badgers from extermination . . .

SAD SONG OF THE WHALE
Tim leaps at the chance to join Green Watch on an anti-whaling expedition. But soon, he and the other members of Green Watch, find themselves shipwrecked and fighting for their lives . . .

DOLPHIN'S REVENGE
The members of Green Watch are convinced that Sam Jefferson is mistreating his dolphins – but how can they prove it? Not only that, but they must save Loner, a wild dolphin, from captivity . . .

MONSTERS ON THE BEACH
The Green Watch team is called to investigate a suspected radiation leak. Teddy McCormack claims to have seen mutated crabs and sea-plants, but there's no proof, and Green Watch don't know whether he's crazy or there's been a cover-up . . .

GORILLA MOUNTAIN
Tim, Brian and Flower fly to Africa to meet the Bests, who are protecting gorillas from poachers. But they are ambushed and Alison Best is kidnapped. It is up to them to rescue her *and* save the gorillas . . .

SPIRIT OF THE CONDOR
Green Watch has gone to California on a surfing holiday – but not for long! Someone is trying to kill the Californian Condor, the bird cherished by an Indian tribe – the Daiku – without which the tribe will die. Green Watch must struggle to save both the Condor and the Daiku . . .

THE BABYSITTERS CLUB

Need a babysitter? Then call the Babysitters Club. Kristy Thomas and her friends are all experienced sitters. They can tackle any job from rampaging toddlers to a pandemonium of pets. To find out all about them, read on!

Look out for: